# THE
# BARNYARD
# BAND

To Marie – J.R.

First published in Great Britain in 1996
by Macmillan Children's Books
a division of Macmillan Publishers Limited
25 Eccleston Place, London SW1W 9NF
and Basingstoke
Associated companies worldwide

ISBN 0 333 62099 2 HB
ISBN 0 333 64758 0 PB

1 3 5 7 9 8 6 4 2

A CIP catalogue record for this book is available
from the British Library

Printed in Hong Kong

# THE BARNYARD BAND

*A story from the Brothers Grimm*
*Retold by James Riordan*

*Illustrated by Charles Fuge*

MACMILLAN CHILDREN'S BOOKS

# ABOUT THIS STORY

In the early 1800s Jakob and Wilhelm Grimm collected folk tales from peasants who lived near the brothers on the middle Rhine in Germany. The stories were written down as they were told, "in the raw"; they weren't altered to make them more acceptable to the society of the day.

After several years of gathering and recording, in 1812, the Grimms published their first collection, when they were still in their mid-twenties. They brought out a second volume two years later, calling the entire collection *Children's and Household Tales*.

*The Barnyard Band* is a retelling of one of their early stories, *The Musicians of Bremen*, which was the twenty-seventh story on the list, out of over two hundred. The original story was put together from two versions, one heard in the Padeborn district and one in Zwehren. Goodness knows how the port of Bremen, on the river Weser – many miles distant – found its way into the tale (perhaps it had a good oompah band at the time); in any case, the animals never did reach it!

In one version, the animals are an ox, a stag, a goat, a fox, a cock and a goose; and the robber mistakes the goose's beak for a pair of red-hot tongs. In another, the "robbers" are a wolf tricked out of his home by the clever animals. In our English version, we have tried to re-create the popular humour of the story through robust language and colourful imagery.

*The Musicians* is, after all, one of the funniest and most colourful tales ever told.

*James Riordan*

An old farmer had a donkey who worked hard for him
down the years without a grumble or a grouse. But now
the donkey's strength was failing, the farmer had no more
use for him and drove him out of the farmyard.

Poor old Ned wandered down the road, thinking he might become a musician in the town. He had long admired his singing voice and now hoped to make a living in a band.

Along the way he came upon a dog lying by the roadside, panting and wheezing.

"Ho, there, Fido," said the donkey. "Why are you puffing like a pair of bellows?"

"Ah," sighed the dog, "you may well ask. Because I'm growing old, my master wants to put me down. So I ran away, though goodness knows how I'll survive."

"I tell you what," said the donkey. "I'm on my way to become a musician. Why don't you come, too? I'll blow the horn, you bang the drum."

The dog willingly fell in with the donkey.  They had not
gone far when they came upon a ginger cat, sitting in the
road with a face as long as a fiddle.

"Now, what's got into you, Ginger?" asked the donkey.

"My mistress says I'm too long in the tooth to catch
mice any more, so she's going to drown me. I ran away to
save my skin."

"Come with us," said the donkey, "and play the
tin whistle in our band."

The cat thought this was a good idea, so she fell in behind the donkey and the dog.

Soon after, the three companions passed a farmyard; and there, standing on the gate, was a cock, crowing at the top of his voice.

"What a hullabaloo!" shouted the donkey. "It's enough to burst your eardrums."

"It's my last crow," groaned the cock. "Just because we've guests coming tomorrow, the farmer's wife intends to chop off my head and cook me for dinner."

"Then come with us," said the donkey. "We're on our way to form a band; you've a fine strong voice, you can be our singer."

The cock was delighted with the idea and fell in behind the others: the donkey, the dog and the cat.

It was a fair walk to town, and by dusk the four friends still had some way to go. They were tired and agreed to spend the night in a wood. The donkey, dog and cat lay down beneath an oak, while the cock flew up into the topmost branches. As he peered around from his lofty perch, he saw a dim light glowing in the distance.

So he passed down the news to the others.

"We'd be cosier in a house for sure," said the donkey. "Let's go and shelter there."

So they made for the light and soon came to a brightly lit
cottage in the middle of a glade. Now, this was the house
of three robbers, and the hideaway where they kept their
gold and stolen treasure.

Since he was the tallest, the donkey went over to the
window and peered inside.

"What can you see? What can you see?" asked the others
eagerly.

"I see a table full of good things to eat and drink,"
he whispered to the others; "and I see three robbers
sitting there."

"That food sounds like it's made for us," said the cock.

"Right you are," said the donkey. "But how are we to scare the men away?"

They put their heads together to work out a plan. And this is what they did.

Old Ned stood by the window. Fido jumped on his back;
Ginger climbed on Fido's back; and the cock flew up and sat
on Ginger's head. When all was ready, Ned gave the signal
and the Barnyard Band struck up a tune.

The cock **crowed**

The dog *howled*

The cat *miaowed*

The donkey **brayed**

And all at the tops of their voices!

Then they all pitched
forward into the room through
the open window with a terrible crash!
What a fright the robbers got! They leapt up in
the air and rushed off helter-skelter into the trees,
certain that a host of demons was chasing them.

How the four musicians laughed. Then they sat down at the table and ate and drank to their hearts' content. When they were full, they blew out the candles and looked for somewhere to sleep.

The donkey chose a warm
dung-heap beside the porch.
    The dog curled up behind
        the door.

The cock flew up to the rafters.
And the cat stretched out upon
the hearth.

When the robbers saw from the trees that the light was out and all seemed calm, the chief scolded his men.

"You lily-livered cowards! Go back at once and see what's going on."

And he sent one robber off to see that the coast was clear.

When the man crept up to the cottage, he found it as quiet as the grave.

Yet, as he entered the kitchen to strike a light, he mistook the eyes of the cat on the hearth for live coals. When he stuck some paper into the coals he had the shock of his life . . .

The cat sprang at his head, spitting
and scratching for all she was worth.
   As the poor man made for the
door, he tripped over the dog,
who bit his leg.

Limping into the yard,
he bumped into the donkey, who gave
his rear a sharp kick, knocking him face down
into the dung.

What with all this racket, the cock woke up, thinking
it was daybreak. "Cock-a-doodle-do! Ku-ku-ree-kee!" he screamed.

More dead than alive, the robber staggered back to his chief and
told him what had happened.

"Lord save us, there's a horrible hag inside the house: she hissed and spat at me and scratched my face with her long nails. Then there's a demon by the door with a knife; he stabbed me in the leg. And in the yard there's a big black monster who struck me an awful blow with a wooden club. Worst of all, there's a policeman on the roof, shouting out, 'Let me thrash him, too! Bring him up to me!' "

On hearing this terrible tale, the robbers all fled for dear life, never going near the place again.

As for the four musicians, they never got to town, and they never really became musicians. The cottage suited them so well they decided to make it their home; after all, it was stocked with food and treasure up to the rafters.

For all I know, they are living there to this day.